The Adventures of
LUCY AND CLARK

The Adventures of
LUCY AND CLARK

The Journey Begins

Erica Cyphert and JoAnna Cyphert

Illustrator Leah Cyphert

gatekeeper press™
TAMPA, FLORIDA

The Adventures of Lucy and Clark: The Journey Begins

Published by Gatekeeper Press
7853 Gunn Hwy, Suite 209
Tampa, FL 33626
www.GatekeeperPress.com

ISBN (hardcover): 9781662931666

ISBN (paperback): 9781662931673

eISBN: 978166293

Dedicated to grandparents everywhere.

Erica Cyphert is a native West Virginian who loves taking her nieces and nephews on adventures to various state and national parks. She enjoys sharing her love of animals, nature and photography. In addition to traveling, Erica loves reading, chocolate and planning adventures.

JoAnna Cyphert is a native of Morgantown, West Virginia. She loves traveling to different states, gardening, watching science fiction and cheering on the West Virginia University Mountaineers.

Leah Cyphert lives in North Carolina with her husband, Luke, their two kids, Mara and Luke, two cats and a chocolate Labrador named Max. Leah loves to travel to the beach, the mountains, amusement parks, historical sites, and the library. When she isn't reading a good book she's thinking up ways to explore all the places and do all the things.

Special thanks to Mara Cyphert for illustrating Clark and Lucy's map.

A young boy's best friend is often his dog. Clark was no different. He and his best friend, Lucy, often played all day. This day they were at Clark's grandparents' farm.

"Go fetch, Lucy." Clark said, as he threw the stick as far as he could across the yard. But Lucy just sat there and looked up at him.

"What's the matter, girl? Tired of playing fetch?" "Woof!" Lucy barked and lay down with her head on her front paws. "Yeah," Clark agreed as he lay down beside Lucy in the grass and looked up at the sky, "I'm tired of that game too."

"What should we do now, Lucy? We already played pirates, explored the banks of the pond for treasures, fought zombies and played fetch. I love coming to visit Grandpa Willard, but sometimes it's hard to come up with things to do when you can't watch TV or play on the computer all day." Lucy looked at Clark as if she agreed completely with her best friend.

Clark's Grandpa Willard was retired but he kept busy with his hobbies and work around the house. Today was no exception, so Clark and Lucy had spent most of the day outside entertaining themselves. Clark loved making up imaginary games involving dragons, dinosaurs or zombies and the heroes who battled them. In his imaginary adventures, he and Lucy were always the heroes who saved the day.

As Grandpa Willard had watched Clark and Lucy race around the front yard, battling some imaginary opponent, he decided to give Clark something that would change the way he and Lucy played forever. It was a gift Grandpa Willard himself had played with as a young boy with his own dog.

Grandpa Willard's mother had been a librarian and she often brought home books for Willard to read. One day, a long time ago, she brought home a big box full of old books that the library was no longer keeping.

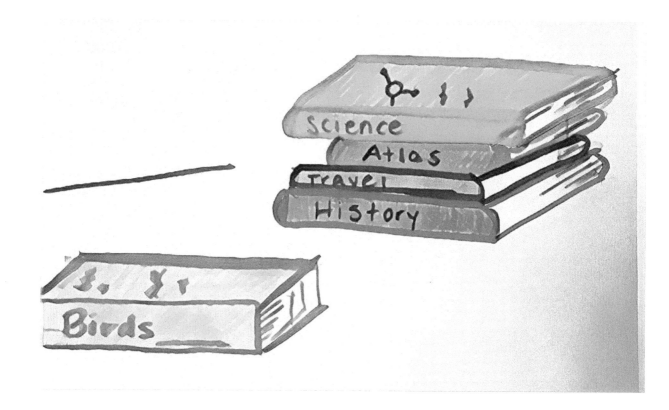

But as every child knows, sometimes playing with the box itself is much more fun than what actually comes in the box. For Grandpa Willard, the box his mother gave him from the library turned out to be one of the best gifts he ever got.

"Did you two run out of things to do already?" Clark heard his Grandpa ask. Clark quickly sat up and saw his Grandpa coming up the stairs from the cellar carrying something large under his arm. "What do you have there, Grandpa?" Clark asked as he and Lucy ran over to him.

"Well, Clark," Grandpa said as he set down a large cardboard box with the word BOOKS written across it in large black letters, "this was one of my favorite toys when I was your age. My mom was a librarian at the bookstore in town where I grew up and one day she brought this box home for me. It was full of old books – history books, math books, books on trees and birds, books on science and travel. I emptied the box, opened the top and bottom and laid it on its side. I called it a travel box and I spent hours having great adventures inside it. I thought you might enjoy playing with it as well.

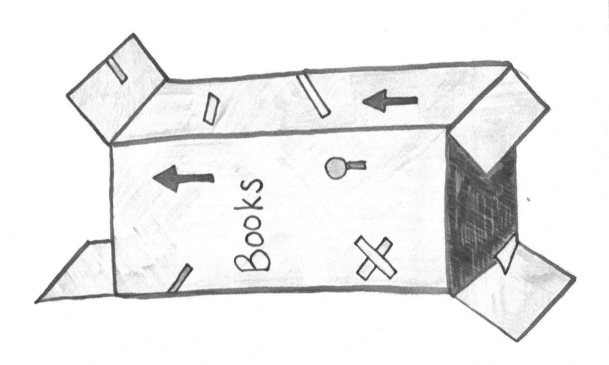

I also have this doggie backpack for Lucy. My dog, Magellan, always wore it when we played with the travel box. "You two have fun now," Grandpa said as he finished strapping the backpack on Lucy. "I need to finish mowing the backyard."

"You look great wearing that backpack, Lucy!" Clark said as he rubbed Lucy's neck and looked at the box Grandpa had given him. The box looked a little beat up and had some duct tape on it in a couple of places. "It has a couple of holes in it," Clark said as he walked around the box, "but we could still pretend it's a fort or boat or something." Lucy let out a loud bark and sniffed her way all around the box, her tail wagging excitedly. Then, she ran inside the box.

"Anything interesting inside, Lucy?" Clark asked as he followed Lucy into the box. "Lucy?" Clark called as he crawled through the box and out through the other end. "Where are you? Whoa," Clark said as he stood up. "Where am I?" Clark had been in Grandpa's front yard when he went into the box but now he was somewhere completely different. Now he was standing on the banks of a lake. As he looked around, Clark realized it was Cooper's Rock Lake. The lake was a part of Cooper's Rock State Forest and it was a whole five miles from his grandparents' house! Clark had been to Cooper's Rock with his Grandpa before to feed the Canadian geese, explore the trails, climb the rock formations and walk out onto the Overlook. "How is this possible?" Clark asked himself out loud.

"I haven't the slightest idea." Clark heard someone say. "Lucy?" Clark asked as he saw his friend walking toward him, still wearing the backpack. "You can talk?" Clark's eyes widened in excitement as he hugged his friend. "You can understand what I'm saying?!" Lucy asked, her voice filled with wonder.

"Apparently the box your Grandpa gave us is not just an ordinary box."

"Do you think Grandpa knows what the box does? Maybe we should go back and ask him about it."

"That," Lucy said, "might be a problem. The box didn't travel with us."

"What? How will we get back?" Clark wondered as he looked all around where they stood.

Before Lucy could answer, one of the Canadian geese floating on the lake flew out of the water and walked over to them. "Hello," the goose said, "what are you two doing here?"

"Well," said Clark, "we aren't quite sure. We were in my Grandpa Willard's front yard playing with a box he gave us and then all of a sudden we were here."

"Grandpa Willard?" the goose asked. "Could it be? I thought I recognized that backpack but I haven't seen it for many years," said the goose, becoming more and more excited. "You must have come through Willard's travel tunnel!"

"A travel tunnel?" said Clark. "I don't know about that. We just crawled through an old box my Grandpa gave us to play with."

"Willard always did call it a travel box," the goose said, rolling his eyes, "but it is obviously a travel tunnel."

"Let me look in your backpack's side pocket," the goose said, "I need to find you something to use with your travel tunnel." Lucy sat still as the goose unzipped the side pocket and pulled out a strange looking pair of round goggles.

"What are these for?" asked Clark as the goose handed him the goggles.

"When you put them on," said the goose, "it makes everything dark except for where you need to go." The goose helped Clark put the goggles on. They were dark like sunglasses and Clark couldn't see anything except for a bright blue light glowing in the distance up on a hill. While keeping the goggles on, Clark was able to flip the outer dark lenses up and could once again see his surroundings but not the glowing blue light.

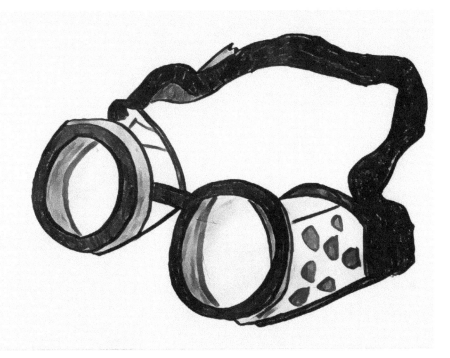

"Now," said the goose, "with the backpack and goggles you can always make it back to the travel tunnel."

"Clark," said Lucy "maybe we can explore Cooper's Rock on our way to the blue light." "Absolutely!" Clark agreed, "This will be a great adventure."

The three had walked a short distance toward the hill when they came across a rabbit eating flowers in a field. "These flowers are delicious," the rabbit said as they passed. "Wow, rabbits talk too," Clark said.

"Wait!" The rabbit said as he stood up, looking puzzled with one ear straight up and one ear bent down. "You can hear what I say?" Lucy walked over to him and said, "You got some of that flower stuck between your teeth."

They all laughed and the goose explained where they were going. The rabbit asked if he could tag along and they all agreed he could.

Clark said, "But I don't see the blue light anywhere." "Me neither," said Lucy. "Flip down the dark glasses on your goggles, Clark," said the goose. Once he did, Clark could again see the glowing blue light coming from the top of the hill.

As the four new friends walked up the hill the rabbit hopped circles around them asking question after question like, "Why can't I see the blue light?" "That's because it can only be seen when wearing the goggles," explained Clark. "It looks like the glowing blue light is coming from one of the trees on top of the hill. Would you like to see?" Clark asked, as he stopped to share his googles with the rabbit so he could see the glowing light before they continued up the hill. "Very interesting. I've never seen anything like it," said the rabbit as he handed the goggles back to Clark and the four new friends continued up the hill.

"There, I see it!" yelled Clark as he pointed to an old tree with a big, thick trunk and lots of branches twisting in different directions. There were no leaves anywhere on the tree and it wasn't like the other spruce trees growing on the hill. The tree's trunk was spilt all the way through at the base so that it looked like it had a giant tunnel going through it. Clark stood on one side of the tree and he could see Lucy and the goose standing on the other side of it.

"You're all set," said the goose as he flapped his wings excitedly. "All you have to do to get back is go through the hole in the tree and you'll be back where you started."

"Thank you for all your help," said Clark. "Yes," Lucy chimed in, "we never would have figured this out without you."

"You're welcome," said the goose. "Just be sure you always wear the backpack Clark's grandpa gave you when you go exploring, Lucy, and remember to use the goggles, Clark." "You still have grass in your teeth," the goose said to the rabbit. The rabbit laughed and used his bent ear to rub between his teeth.

Lucy raced through the hole and Clark quickly followed her. When they came out the other side they were back in the front yard of grandpa and grandma's house, right by the box grandpa had given them. "Wow, what an amazing adventure! Can you believe what we just did?" Clark asked Lucy. "Woof!" Lucy barked excitedly, wagging her tail rapidly.

"Did you two have a good afternoon?" grandpa asked as he came around the side of the house. "Grandpa!" Clark yelled excitedly as he and Lucy ran toward him. "You'll never believe what happened. The box you gave me isn't just a box; it's a tunnel!"

"Slow down and take a breath, Clark," grandpa said as he scratched Lucy's neck. "Your mom is here and she's ready to go home."

"Already?" asked Clark with his head down and shoulders slumped. Clark raised his head and looked hopefully at his grandpa. "Grandpa," he whispered, "do you think I could play with your travel tunnel the next time I come to visit?"

"Well," said grandpa thoughtfully, "I suppose you could. Or, you could take it home with you. That way, you and Lucy can play with it any time you like. What do you think?"

"Really?" Clark asked as his face lit up. "Thanks Grandpa! You're the best!! I'll take great care of it."

"I'm sure you will, Clark," Grandpa said. "Just remember, you can never get rid of it."

"Don't worry, Grandpa," Clark said as he gave his grandpa a big hug, "I'll keep it forever."

Clark picked up the box as he and Lucy walked toward his mom's car and said, "We're going to take lots of adventures, Lucy, and become great explorers. When we get home I'm going to draw a map of where we explored today. That way, we can keep a journal of all our adventures." Lucy wagged her tail and jumped into the back of the car.

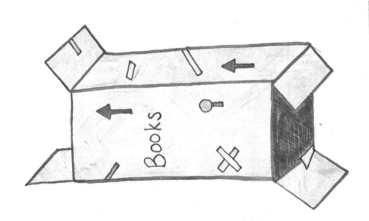